Who Spilled That Stuff?

Who Spilled That Stuff?

V. Gilbert Beers

Illustrated by Tonda Rae Nalle

VICTOR BOOKS

A DIVISION OF SCRIPTURE PRESS PUBLICATIONS INC.
USA CANADA ENGLAND

Published in Wheaton, Illinois by Victor Books/SP Publications, Inc.,
Wheaton, Illinois

ISBN 1-56476-316-1

Printed in the United States of America

1 2 3 4 5 6 — 00 99 98 97 96 95

TO PARENTS AND TEACHERS

What does your child do when a problem comes along? How does she respond to it? Where does he find the solution?

What we need is a good role model—someone who faces problems as we do, but knows the right way to resolve them. The Muffin Family is a role-model family. They face problems much like the ones that bother us daily. But there's a difference. The Muffins are not quite like their neighbors. You will soon learn that they are Christians, and thus they meet their problems with Bible truth.

The Muffins aren't perfect. Neither are you and I. But they are Christian. They aren't free from problems. But they resolve them—God's Way.

If you're looking for a book that will role-model Bible truth at work in a family much like yours, meet The Muffin Family.

V. Gilbert Beers

"Who spilled the antifreeze?" Poppi grumbled. Mommi looked surprised and hurt.

"I haven't seen your antifreeze," she answered. "I don't even know where your antifreeze is and I don't care who spilled it."

Mommi was angry. Poppi was accusing her of something she had not done. She hadn't spilled anything, especially his antifreeze.

"Well, someone spilled my gallon jug of antifreeze," Poppi complained. "I set it by the work bench. Then I stepped out of the garage for three minutes, and zap, someone spilled it."

Mommi and Poppi Muffin
didn't argue very often. So
Mommi decided not to talk
anymore about antifreeze. That is,
she didn't talk anymore about it
until Maxi walked into the
kitchen where Mommi was
angrily washing some dishes.

Almost without thinking, Mommi snapped at Maxi, "Who spilled that antifreeze?"

"That what?" Maxi asked. He was surprised to hear Mommi talking about antifreeze.

"I haven't been near your antifreeze. I didn't know you had any. And if I had known it, I certainly wouldn't have spilled it."

Now both Mommi and Maxi were hurt, surprised, and angry. Maxi stomped into the living room. Seeing Mini curled up comfortable on the sofa with a book made Maxi even more angry.

"Who spilled that antifreeze?" Maxi demanded. Mini almost dropped her book.

"What's anty freeze?" Mini asked innocently.

"Never mind what it is," Maxi snapped. "I'm asking who spilled it?"

Mini looked surprised and hurt. "How can I tell you who spilled it if I don't even know what the stuff is?" Mini asked.

Now Mini was angry. She slammed the door as she went outside.

Mini was even more angry when Ruff came bounding up to her. He was ready to play, but Mini didn't feel like playing.

"You spilled that anty freeze!" Mini shouted at Ruff. Ruff stopped looking happy and playful. He put his tail between his legs and hung his head. Then Ruff looked up at Mini with big, sad, brown eyes. He waited to see what Mini would say next.

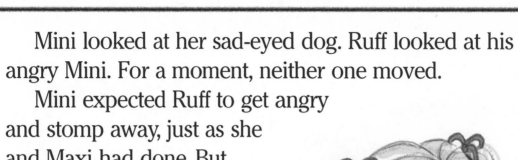

Mini looked at her sad-eyed dog. Ruff looked at his angry Mini. For a moment, neither one moved.

Mini expected Ruff to get angry and stomp away, just as she and Maxi had done. But instead, Ruff began to wag just the tip of his tail.

How could Mini stay angry when he did that? She threw her arms around Ruff and a big tear ran down her cheek. Now his whole tail wagged back and forth.

"Oh, Ruff, why did I yell at you?" Mini whispered. "You forgave me even before I asked."

Then Mini knew what she must do. She must forgive Maxi and smile at him, just as Ruff had done to her.

Mini ran into the house and tapped on Maxi's bedroom door.

Maxi still looked angry when he opened the door. "Well, what do you want?" he yelled at Mini. Maxi stopped yelling when he saw Mini smiling at him.

"Maxi, I just want you to know that I love you," she said softly. "And I forgive you."

Maxi stared at Mini. How could he stay angry at her now?

"I guess I love you too," he said slowly.

"I'm really sorry I said what I did. You're forgiving me even before I ask. And I don't deserve it."

Maxi walked down to the kitchen and found Mommi, still angrily washing dishes. When Mommi heard Maxi come into the room, she turned around, looking upset.

Before Mommi could say anything, she saw Maxi smiling at her.

"I love you, Mommi," Maxi said. "And I forgive you."

Mommi stared at Maxi. How could she stay angry at him now? Anyway, she couldn't think of any good reason to be angry at Maxi.

Mommi threw her arms around Maxi and gave him a big hug. "I love you too, Maxi," she said as a tear ran down her face. "Here you are, forgiving me before I even ask you to. But now I'm asking you to forgive me."

"Oh, sure, Mommi," Maxi answered. He knew exactly how she felt.

As Maxi went back to his room, he whistled cheerfully. He even looked happily at Mini curled up on the sofa with her book.

Mommi stood by the kitchen sink for a moment, wondering what to do next. Then she went out to the garage. There was Poppi, mopping up the last of the antifreeze.

26

Poppi was still angry when he looked up and saw Mommi come into the garage. He almost snapped at Mommi again.

Then he saw a beautiful smile on her face. "I love you, honey," Mommi whispered. "And I forgive you."

Poppi stood there holding a bunch of messy rags. How could he be angry at Mommi now?

Poppi dumped the rags into a garbage bag, cleaned his hands and gave Mommi a big hug and kiss.

"I love you too!" Poppi said softly. "Thank you for forgiving me, even before I asked you. I'm sorry for accusing you."

Mommi and Poppi walked to the house, holding hands and laughing. Maxi and Mini smiled as they watched from the kitchen window.

"Who did spill the anty freeze?" Mini asked Poppi at dinner.

Poppi chuckled. "I probably did by accident," he said. "But that antifreeze taught us all something important."

"The anty freeze didn't teach us," Mini said. "Ruff did!" Then she told how Ruff's wagging tail started the chain of forgiveness.

"So Ruff deserves a special medal," Poppi said. He cut out a big red heart from construction paper, tied a string to it and hung it around Ruff's neck. On the heart it said "HERO." How do you think Ruff felt when he saw that?